# The Magic Word

First published in 2007 by
Franklin Watts
338 Euston Road
London
NW1 3BH

Franklin Watts Australia
Level 17/207 Kent Street
Sydney
NSW 2000



A CIP catalogue record for this book is available from the British Library.

ISBN 978 0 7496 7096 2 (hbk)
ISBN 978 0 7496 7800 5 (pbk)

**Series Editor:** Jackie Hamley
**Editor:** Melanie Palmer
**Series Advisor:** Dr Barrie Wade
**Series Designer:** Peter Scoulding

Printed in China

Franklin Watts is a division of
Hachette Children's Books,
an Hachette Livre UK company.

# The Magic Word

by Maggie Moore

Illustrated by Martin Remphry

One hot day, a cloud of buzzing flies flew into the royal palace.

"Send for Merlin the Magician," said the King. "He will make them disappear!"

Merlin sent his boy, Mervin,

to the palace instead.

Mervin was learning
to be a magician.

Mervin waved his
magic wand.
"Buzz off, flies!" he said.
"AB..."

But the flies turned into scuttling spiders.

"Try again," said the King.

So Mervin waved his
magic wand again.
"Scuttle off, spiders,"
he said. "AB-RA..."

But the spiders turned into hopping frogs.

"Oh dear!" cried the King,

"Try again."

Again, Mervin waved his magic wand.
"Hop off, frogs," he said.
"AB-RA-CAD..."

But the frogs turned into scrambling monkeys.

"Oh, no!" cried the King.
"Quick! Try again!"

Once more, Mervin waved his magic wand.
"Scramble off, monkeys," he said. "AB-RA-CAD-AB..."

But the monkeys turned into lumbering elephants.

“Help!” yelled the King.

This time everybody helped. Mervin waved his wand and said: "Lumber off elephants!"

Then everyone shouted:

All the elephants disappeared.

“Well done, Mervin!” said the King.

**Leapfrog has been specially designed to fit the requirements of the National Literacy Strategy. It offers real books for beginning readers by top authors and illustrators. There are 67 Leapfrog stories to choose from:**

**The Bossy Cockerel**
ISBN 978 0 7496 3828 3

**Bill's Baggy Trousers**
ISBN 978 0 7496 3829 0

**Little Joe's Big Race**
ISBN 978 0 7496 3832 0

**The Little Star**
ISBN 978 0 7496 3833 7

**The Cheeky Monkey**
ISBN 978 0 7496 3830 6

**Selfish Sophie**
ISBN 978 0 7496 4385 0

**Recycled!**
ISBN 978 0 7496 4388 1

**Felix on the Move**
ISBN 978 0 7496 4387 4

**Pippa and Poppa**
ISBN 978 0 7496 4386 7

**Jack's Party**
ISBN 978 0 7496 4389 8

**The Best Snowman**
ISBN 978 0 7496 4390 4

**Mary and the Fairy**
ISBN 978 0 7496 4633 2

**The Crying Princess**
ISBN 978 0 7496 4632 5

**Jasper and Jess**
ISBN 978 0 7496 4081 1

**The Lazy Scarecrow**
ISBN 978 0 7496 4082 8

**The Naughty Puppy**
ISBN 978 0 7496 4383 6

**Big Bad Blob**
ISBN 978 0 7496 7092 4*
ISBN 978 0 7496 7796 1

**Cara's Breakfast**
ISBN 978 0 7496 7093 1*
ISBN 978 0 7496 7797 8

**Why Not?**
ISBN 978 0 7496 7094 8*
ISBN 978 0 7496 7798 5

**Croc's Tooth**
ISBN 978 0 7496 7095 5*
ISBN 978 0 7496 7799 2

**The Magic Word**
ISBN 978 0 7496 7096 2*
ISBN 978 0 7496 7800 5

**Tim's Tent**
ISBN 978 0 7496 7097 9*
ISBN 978 0 7496 7801 2

**FAIRY TALES**

**Cinderella**
ISBN 978 0 7496 4228 0

**The Three Little Pigs**
ISBN 978 0 7496 4227 3

**Jack and the Beanstalk**
ISBN 978 0 7496 4229 7

**The Three Billy Goats Gruff**
ISBN 978 0 7496 4226 6

**Goldilocks and the Three Bears**
ISBN 978 0 7496 4225 9

**Little Red Riding Hood**
ISBN 978 0 7496 4224 2

**Rapunzel**
ISBN 978 0 7496 6159 5

**Snow White**
ISBN 978 0 7496 6161 8

**The Emperor's New Clothes**
ISBN 978 0 7496 6163 2

**The Pied Piper of Hamelin**
ISBN 978 0 7496 6164 9

**Hansel and Gretel**
ISBN 978 0 7496 6162 5

**The Sleeping Beauty**
ISBN 978 0 7496 6160 1

**Rumpelstiltskin**
ISBN 978 0 7496 6165 6

**The Ugly Duckling**
ISBN 978 0 7496 6166 3

**Puss in Boots**
ISBN 978 0 7496 6167 0

**The Frog Prince**
ISBN 978 0 7496 6168 7

**The Princess and the Pea**
ISBN 978 0 7496 6169 4

**Dick Whittington**
ISBN 978 0 7496 6170 0

**The Elves and the Shoemaker**
ISBN 978 0 7496 6581 4

**The Little Match Girl**
ISBN 978 0 7496 6582 1

**The Little Mermaid**
ISBN 978 0 7496 6583 8

**The Little Red Hen**
ISBN 978 0 7496 6585 2

**The Nightingale**
ISBN 978 0 7496 6586 9

**Thumbelina**
ISBN 978 0 7496 6587 6

**RHYME TIME**

**Mr Spotty's Potty**
ISBN 978 0 7496 3831 3

**Eight Enormous Elephants**
ISBN 978 0 7496 4634 9

**Freddie's Fears**
ISBN 978 0 7496 4382 9

**Squeaky Clean**
ISBN 978 0 7496 6805 1

**Craig's Crocodile**
ISBN 978 0 7496 6806 8

**Felicity Floss: Tooth Fairy**
ISBN 978 0 7496 6807 5

**Captain Cool**
ISBN 978 0 7496 6808 2

**Monster Cake**
ISBN 978 0 7496 6809 9

**The Super Trolley Ride**
ISBN 978 0 7496 6810 5

**The Royal Jumble Sale**
ISBN 978 0 7496 6811 2

**But, Mum!**
ISBN 978 0 7496 6812 9

**Dan's Gran's Goat**
ISBN 978 0 7496 6814 3

**Lighthouse Mouse**
ISBN 978 0 7496 6815 0

**Big Bad Bart**
ISBN 978 0 7496 6816 7

**Ron's Race**
ISBN 978 0 7496 6817 4

**Woolly the Bully**
ISBN 978 0 7496 7098 6*
ISBN 978 0 7496 7790 9

**Boris the Spider**
ISBN 978 0 7496 7099 3*
ISBN 978 0 7496 7791 6

**Miss Polly's Seaside Brolly**
ISBN 978 0 7496 7100 6*
ISBN 978 0 7496 7792 3

**The Lonely Pirate**
ISBN 978 0 7496 7101 3*
ISBN 978 0 7496 7793 0

**What a Frog!**
ISBN 978 0 7496 7102 0*
ISBN 978 0 7496 7794 7

**Juggling Joe**
ISBN 978 0 7496 7103 7*
ISBN 978 0 7496 7795 4

* hardback